Little Animal Activity Book

by
Nina Barbaresi

DOVER PUBLICATIONS, INC., New York

Little Animal Activity Book is a new work, first published by Dover Publications, Inc., in 1990.

International Standard Book Number: 0-486-26272-3

Manufactured in the United States of America
Dover Publications, Inc., 31 East 2nd Street, Mineola, N.Y. 11501

Note

The activities in this book are centered around friendly little animals who are eager for you to recognize them, call them by name, and play with them! They await you in 40 games and puzzles: crossword, follow-the-dots, color-by-number, search-a-word, and many more of your favorites. As you color, spell, count, draw, and do all the other things that these activities will demand, you'll be involved with animals all the time—identifying them, spelling their names, and remembering some of their special features and habits. After you complete a puzzle, you can check your work with the Solutions that begin on page 53. And while you're getting acquainted with the animals, you can color them too!

Mama Dinosaur has lost her four little ones. Can you help her find them?

4

What does each of these animals have that it shouldn't?

Count up all the dogs in this odd but friendly group, and circle the correct number at the bottom of the page.

Find the three animals in this picture whose names begin with the letter A.

7

Which three of the things surrounding Peter remind him of the Fourth of July?

DON + [key] = [tiger]

[tie] + GER = [porcupine]

PORK + U + [tree] = [donkey]

Read out loud the things in each group on the left, whether they are letters or pictures, and in each case you will say the name of an animal. Then draw a line from the word to that animal.

Rusty is at home on the range, but three things look mighty funny. Can you find them?

Ruth is looking for a pair of matching mittens. Help her to pick them out.

H	O	P	I	G
M	T	W	R	D
I	T	F	E	U
S	E	O	A	C
A	R	X	D	K

OTTER

Look at the animals and their names on the opposite page. Then find their names hidden in the grid above and circle them, just the way the word "otter" is circled.

12

DUCK

FOX

PIG

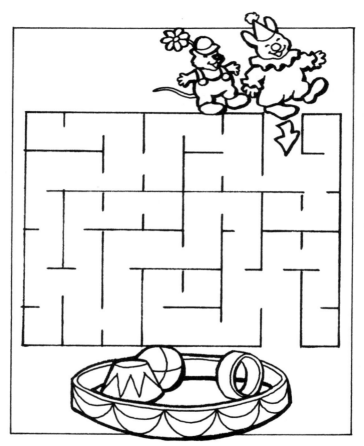

Don't keep the audience at the circus waiting! Lead these two silly clowns to the ring, so the show can go on.

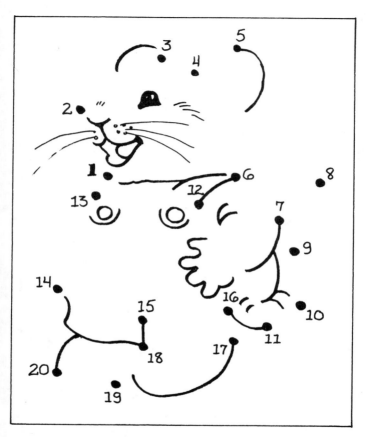

What kind of little animal is this? Find out by connecting dots 1 through 20.

1

D
2 I N [ ] [ ]
N
O
S
A
3 [ ] 4 [ ] R [ ]

To do the crossword puzzle on the opposite page, spell out the names of the things on this page. The numbers next to the pictures tell you where the names belong in the puzzle.

Find the three animals in this picture whose names begin with the letter B.

Marie wants to eat the ice cream cone before it melts.
Hurry her through this maze, or she will be too late!

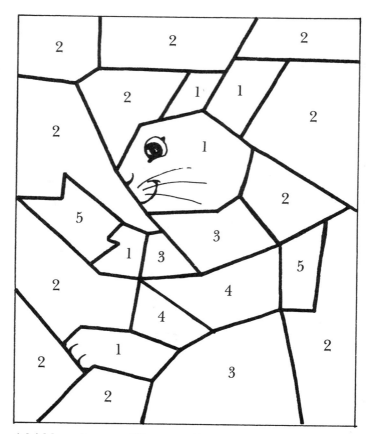

A hidden picture will appear if you color the numbered spaces as follows: (1) light brown; (2) green; (3) yellow; (4) red; (5) leave these spaces white.

20

Clang clang! Help the brave firefighters over the winding roads to reach the fire. Hurry!

O	W	L	A	B
W	H	I	G	U
D	E	M	O	L
R	S	E	A	L
B	L	I	T	H

GOAT

Look at the animals and their names on the opposite page. Then find those names hidden in the grid above and circle them, just the way the word "goat" is circled.

SEAL

OWL

BULL

23

While Claude has been asleep, three strange things have appeared in his room. Can you see them?

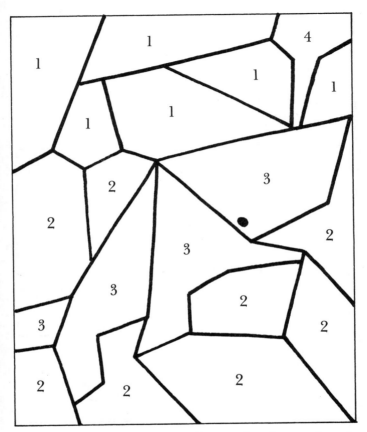

A hidden picture will appear if you color the numbered spaces as follows: (1) blue; (2) dark green; (3) gray; (4) leave this space white.

To do this crossword puzzle, spell out the names of the animals on the opposite page. The numbers next to the pictures tell you where the names belong in the puzzle.

Which three of the things surrounding Danny remind him of Thanksgiving?

Read out loud the things in each group on the left, whether they are letters or pictures, and in each case you will say the name of an animal. Then draw a line from the word to that animal.

In each picture on these two pages, an animal is showing off an object. The animal's name rhymes with the object's name. Write the rhyming names side by side in the spaces next to each picture.

These little animals are hungry! Draw a line from each animal to the food it likes to eat.

These little creatures are homesick! Draw a line from
each one to the place where it lives.

33

Look carefully at these two pictures of Bea and Barney at the beach. Can you find the six ways that the pictures differ?

Find the three animals in this picture whose names begin with the letter C.

Wanda is all dressed up for Halloween. Do you see three
things that might be awaiting her on that spooky night?

How many birds are flying around in this picture?
Count them and circle the correct number.

Among all these shoes, Melissa is trying to find one pair to wear. Help her to find two shoes that match.

Look carefully at these two pictures of a birthday party. Can you find the six ways that they differ?

Which three of the things pictured here would Rachel
see at Christmastime?

It's Wayne's first day at a new school! Guide him along
the road that leads to the school grounds.

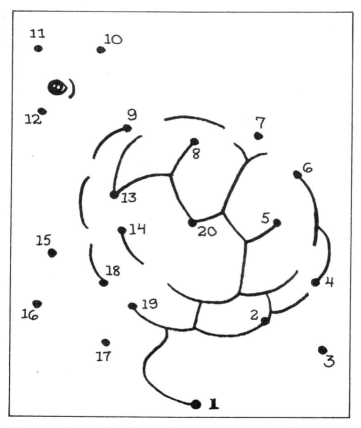

To reveal the identity of this armored animal, connect dots 1 through 20.

Where do these animals live? Draw a line from each one
to its home.

Find the three animals in this picture whose names begin with the letter D.

Cory has two winter hats that look exactly alike. Which are they?

Does something look funny to you about each of these animals?

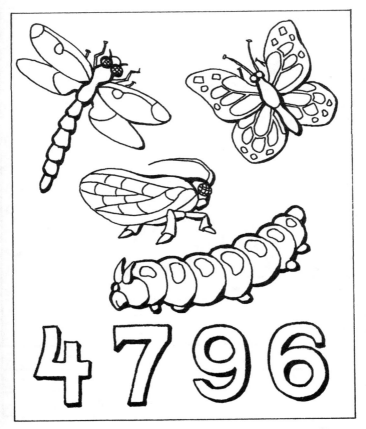

Count all the insects in this picture, whether they fly or crawl, and circle the correct number.

In each of the pictures on these two pages, the animals are showing off objects. The names of the objects rhyme

with the names of the animals. Write the rhyming names side by side in the spaces next to each picture.

Solutions

page 4

page 5

page 6

page 7

page 8

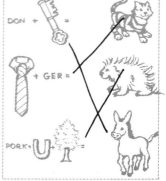

page 9

page 10

page 12

page 11

page 14

OTTER

H	O	P	I	G
M	T	W	R	D
I	T	F	E	U
S	E	O	A	C
A	R	X	D	K

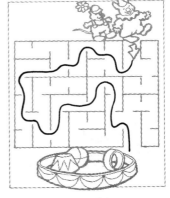

55

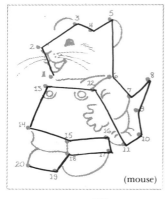

page 15

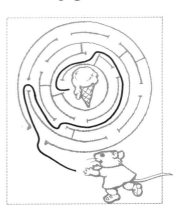

page 16

page 18

page 19

page 20

page 21

page 22

page 24

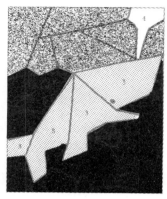

page 25

page 26

page 28

page 29

page 30

page 31

page 32

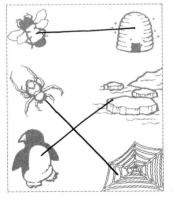

page 33

page 35

page 36

page 37

page 38

60

page 39

page 41

page 42

page 43

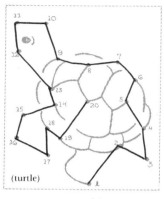

page 44

page 45

page 46

page 47

62

page 48

page 49

page 50

page 51